Square-Eyed Raccoon

Home Sweet Home!

Written by
Sylvia Melanson

Illustrations by
Lynda Melanson

auteuresmelanson.ca

**It all started
one spring night.**
I quietly tiptoed to my burrow
when the moon came out.
The air was fresh. I took the time
to admire the lovely houses.

Suddenly,
a vast cat emerged
in front of me.
I had met street cats in my life,
but this one was **huge!**

Dainty lady as I was,
I climbed up onto the roof
of the nearest house to
escape its muddy claws.

From the roof,
I saw the shaggy cat
keeping a close watch on me.
**This was not the time
for me to go back down!**

It was quite comfortable up there,
on top of the little white house.
The sun's rays had left a
pleasant warmth on the roof.
I had always been fond of this house.
I even imagined myself
living there one day.

Suddenly,

the cat started meowing,
loud enough to wake up
the lady of the house.
She glanced out her bedroom window.
I froze and stiffened
every muscle of my body.
My life was over!
Surprisingly, the lady did not see me.
She closed the curtains
and went back to bed.

The scruffy cat kept
wandering near the house.
So, I decided to stay up
there for a while and
study the stars.

As I walked around the roof
to admire the view,
I saw a tiny door leading to the attic.
This door had a metal vent
attached in the middle.
Curious, I moved forward to inspect it.

I noticed a space
between the door and the vent.
The kind of space that screamed
at me to slide my hand in.
So, I slipped in my skillful fingers,
bent the metal plate,
and smoothly sneaked into the attic.
Home at last!

The interior was strangely decorated. There were yellow and pink puffy blankets that did not suit my taste. But I had found the perfect place to have a family, children, many children, and more children. It was paradise on earth! I snuggled up into a corner and took a **long nap.**

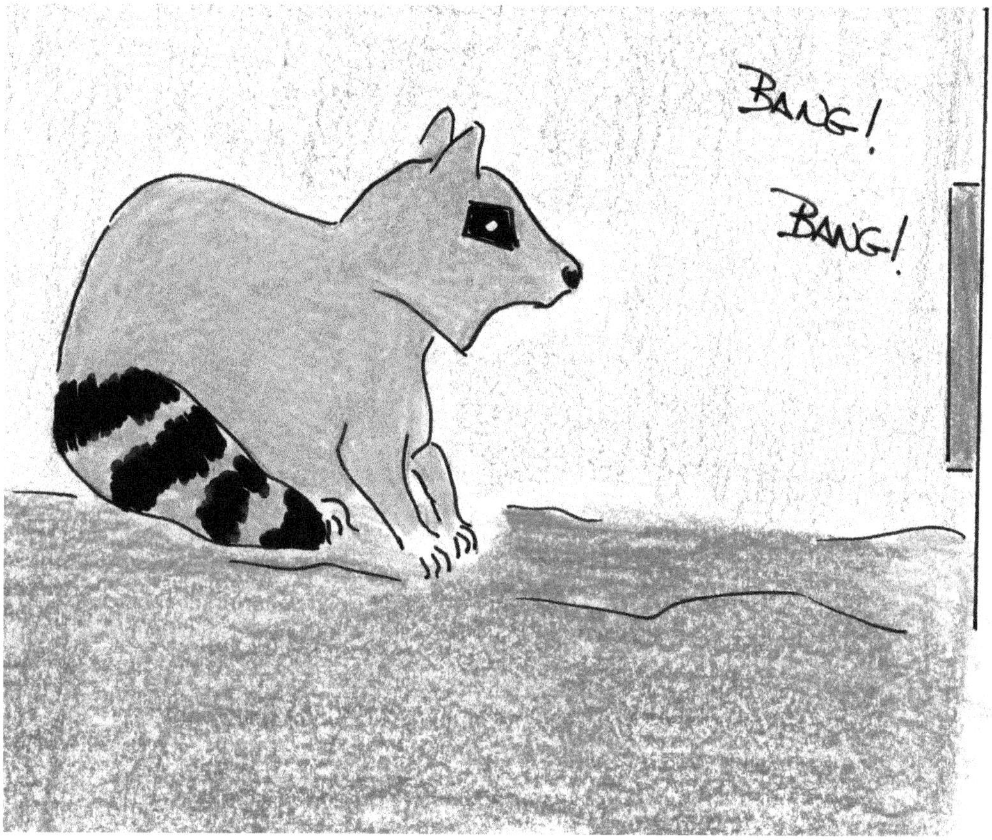
BANG!
BANG!

In the morning,
there were bangs on the metal vent.
The lady of the house was repairing the vent.
She did not know I was inside the attic.
Then I heard her car start.
The car rolled down her pebbled driveway,
and she drove away.

Soon, I realized I was locked in.
I had to get out!
I was good at pulling
or knocking things over,
but I could not push
the little door open.

So, I started scratching around the vent.

I knew it would take hours,
even weeks, for me to see daylight.
I continued to scratch and
munch on the door until sunset.

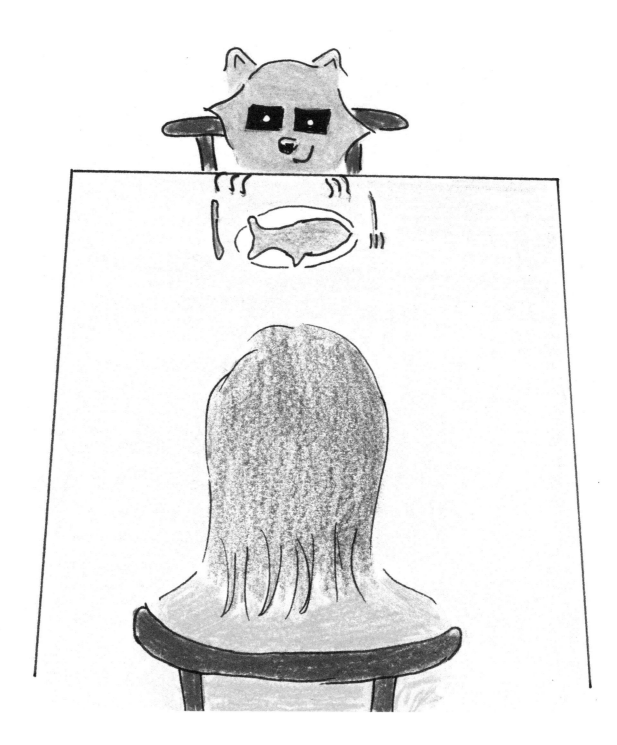

In the evening,

the lady climbed a ladder
and unlocked the little door.
She had heard me nibbling the metal vent.
She knew I had moved in.
I told myself we would become good friends.
We would share meals,
and I would bring fresh fish
from the Yellow River.

Unfortunately, my dreams shattered
when a beam of light dazzled me.
And when the lady yelled,
**"Get out of there,
you square-eyed raccoon!"**

I rushed to the back of the attic
to escape the blazing light.
What did she mean by **square-eyed?**
This episode was surprising.

My brain was having trouble translating two words in Raccoonish: **square and eyed**.
I knew this was not the time to play guessing games. Instead, I needed to keep the lady far away from me until she gave up her hunting game. Which she did, at last.

When everything became quiet,
I crawled out of the attic
and down from the roof.
I was hoping the ragged
cat was not nearby.
I peacefully tiptoed to
my old shelter, thinking,
I will return tomorrow and move back
into the attic of the little white house.

 FriesenPress

Suite 300 - 990 Fort St
Victoria, BC, V8V 3K2
Canada

www.friesenpress.com

ISBN
978-1-5255-8593-7 (Hardcover)
978-1-5255-8592-0 (Paperback)
978-1-5255-8594-4 (eBook)

1. JUVENILE FICTION, ANIMALS, MAMMALS

Distributed to the trade by The Ingram Book Company

auteuresmelanson.ca

CPSIA information can be obtained
at www.ICGtesting.com
Printed in the USA
BVHW020404161220
595677BV00039B/523